# Grief is Like a Snowflake

published by

**National Center for Youth Issues**

Practical Guidance Resources
Educators Can Trust

www.ncyi.org

*A special dedication to Anna,*
*Ben, Trenton and Jackson.*

*–Love, Julia*

## This book is brought to you by the following:

### The Kim Foundation

### Grateful Owl, LLC

### Arbor Family Counseling

### Dr. Michael and Rosanna Morris

**a gift in memory of**
**Victoria and Sylvia Buskuhl**
*and*

Ted E. Bear Hollow
*Mending the hearts of grieving children and teens*

### Ted E. Bear Hollow

## Duplication and Copyright

**National Center for Youth Issues**
ncyi.org
Practical Guidance Resources
Educators Can Trust

P.O. Box 22185 • Chattanooga, TN 37422-2185 • 423.899.5714 • 866.318.6294 • fax: 423.899.4547
www.ncyi.org
ISBN: 978-1-931636-78-0  US $9.95
© 2011 National Center for Youth Issues, Chattanooga, TN
All rights reserved.
Written by: Julia Cook • Illustrations by: Anita DuFalla • Design by: Phillip W. Rodgers
Published by National Center for Youth Issues
Softcover
Printed at RR Donnelley, Inc • Reynosa, Mexico • June 2017

Deep in the emerald forest grew a beautiful little pine tree.
He was very, very sad. He was so sad that he cried tree sap tears every day.
He cried so much that he was almost out of tree sap tears…
A few weeks ago, his father was taken.

"Why my dad?" the little pine tree asked his mom.
"Why was my dad the one?"

"I don't know why," said his mom. "It just happened."

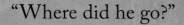

"Where did he go?"

"We won't find that out until it is our time to go," she said.

"Will he ever come back?"

"His trunk, branches and pine needles are gone now,
and they will never come back. But his roots are still hugging yours,
and his memory will live inside of your heart forever."

"But if he's not coming back, who will protect me from the cold winter wind?"

"I will," said the momma tree.
"I will," said the uncle tree.
"We all will," said the emerald forest.

"When it is summer time, who will shade me when the sun is too hot for my needles?"

"I will," said the momma tree.
"I will," said the uncle tree.
"We all will," said the emerald forest.

"I just can't believe that he's gone. I feel like somebody cut off all my branches and now I am just an empty stick stuck in the ground."

"I know how you feel on the inside. I feel like a lightning bolt split me in half."

"Where will the cardinal family build their nest?"

"I'm sure they will find the right place."

"My dad's top branch was the right place. There will never be a better place for their nest than his branch.

Now he's gone and now the cardinal family is leaving, too."

"You look pretty sad for a Christmas tree,"
a flocked tree said to the daddy pine tree next to him.

"Look at me! I am beautiful and I was covered in lights and I have
plastic snow and I was decorated with beautiful ornaments and I had
tons of presents underneath me. I was the most beautiful Christmas
tree on the block. Look! I'm still wearing one of my ornaments."

"That's nice," said the daddy pine tree.

"I can see that they didn't give you plastic snow, but did you have beautiful lights?"

"No."

"Did you get to wear ornaments like this one?"

"No."

"Did people put fancy presents underneath you?"

"No."

"Like I said, you must have looked pretty sad for a Christmas tree."

"Actually, I was a beautiful tree. I was covered in paper chains that were made by love. Each link of my paper chain had a message written from a child to a loved one who died. My pine cones were pulled off of me, decorated with glitter, and given away as presents. I made a lot of people smile.

Besides, none of the stuff that you are mumbling about really matters."

"What?"

"Plastic snow, fancy lights, beautifully wrapped presents…
what really matters in life is what is on the inside. How is your mulch?"

"My mulch?"

"Yes, your mulch. Your mulch is the stuff that is inside of your heart.
It's what you give back to others."

"Maybe if I'm really good and I do everything I'm told, my daddy will come back."

"I wish he would come back little tree, but no matter how good you are that is not going to happen."

**"But it's not FAIR!**
Why me? Why us?
Why our family?"

**"You're right. It isn't fair,**
it isn't fair at all, but we can't change what happened.

I wish I had the answers to all of your questions, but I don't.

What I do know is that I love you with all of my heart.

We have to work together to try to get through this."

"Are you going to be taken away, too?"

"I can't promise you that I won't be taken away, but I will do my very best to take care of us. I will do everything I can to keep our family safe and healthy."

"How come you don't cry?
Don't you feel bad?
Don't you miss him, too?"

"Oh son, I do cry. I cry every single day.
I cry on the inside.

Grief is like a snowflake.
Each snowflake is different
and everyone shows
grief differently.

Just like snow, sometimes grief comes one flake at a time.
Other times it comes like a blizzard. It melts away, but
then it always comes back.

You cry sap tears on the outside.

I cry sap tears on the inside.

Your uncle is so sad he has stopped drinking the rain water, and now his needles are starting to fall off.

The whole emerald forest makes sad noises when the wind blows. Everyone misses your daddy.

What you do need to know is that
it's ok for you to be sad.

It's ok for you
to be mad.

It's ok for you to feel everyway that you feel.
Just remember, you can always talk to me about how you are feeling.
No feeling that you have is too big or too small for us to talk about."

"I don't want to talk to you
or anybody right now.

I just want to be
with my dad."

"What really matters in life is not what you get…it's what you give back," the daddy pine tree said to the flocked tree. "You were given plastic snow, fancy lights, and beautiful presents, but all of those things have to be stripped away from you before you can enter the 'Great Equalizer.'

The 'Great Equalizer' only cares about what your insides are made of. That's what you give back.

Have you ever offered your branch to a real cardinal family so that they could build their nest?"

"No."

"Believe me, the soft feathers of a real bird feel much better against your needles than this hard plastic thing does.

Have you ever offered warmth
from the cold winter wind,

or shade from the
hot summer sun to a
younger tree?"

"No."

"Have you ever given your pine cones away as presents?"

"No."

"Believe me, there is no better feeling in the world than giving of yourself and being there for someone who really needs you."

"Your daddy is gone.  I know how much you miss him.
I miss him too, but I promise you, little tree, your daddy is still in your life.
He will always be in your life."

"I'm afraid that I might forget him."

"You will never be able to forget him because he is a part of you.
In time, he will find a way to show you that."

**Ted E. Bear Hollow**

*Mending the hearts of grieving children and teens*

# "Ted E. Bear" Tips

Here are some helpful hints for adults supporting grieving children.

**T – Tell the truth.** Be honest when talking to children about the death. Though they may not need to know all the details, it is important for them to receive truthful explanations. Do not lie about the death. In case you don't have an answer, it's ok to say, "I don't know".

**E – Explain concretely.** Children aren't able to process figurative language like adults. Say "died" rather than "passed away", "lost", or "went to sleep". Explain that when someone dies, he or she no longer needs to eat, sleep, or go to the bathroom.

**D – Don't deny.** It is okay for children to see you cry or to let them know how you are feeling. If you deny or try to hide your emotions in front of them, they are likely to hide theirs as well.

**E – Expect many emotions.** Grieving children will experience a variety of emotions including sadness, anger, guilt, confusion, jealousy, and even happiness. Let them know that it is normal to feel however they are feeling. Expect these emotions to come and go quickly. They may be crying one moment and playing the next.

**B – Be all ears.** It is important for children to tell their story and express their emotions. Check in with them regularly and let them know you are there to listen. Ask open-ended questions and let them do the talking.

**E – Encourage play.** Play is a normal and healthy outlet for children. It is not uncommon for young children to play funeral or heaven, much like playing school or house. Encourage activities that help children express their emotions. See our accompanying activity book for suggestions.

**A – Allow choices.** Following a death, a child's world will feel out of control. Offering choices will help children regain some sense of control and promotes a healthy grief experience.

**R – Routine.** Because of this "out of control" feeling, it is also important to maintain a routine as much as possible. This provides children a sense of stability and security and reassures them that the adults in their lives will continue to take care of them.

## www.tedebearhollow.org

**Our Mission:** Ted E. Bear Hollow provides a safe and loving environment where grieving children and their families can recognize and honor their feelings of loss and grief through support and education. Support groups and camps are offered free of charge to families.